For B

can
the mounta
where we meet,
Lots of love,
Helen
x x x

The mountains in our hearts

Written and illustrated by Helen Patuck

Edited and reviewed by Dr. Usama Alshughry,
Dr. Fiona Flinn and Dr. Hassan Regan

This book was first printed in London in September 2021, by Kitabna - Our Book CIC

ISBN: 978-1-9162176-7-6

www.kitabna.org

Our book for newcomers

Kitabna means "our book" in Arabic. This therapeutic story was created for newcomer children arriving in the UK and Ireland to start a new life, especially in Northern Ireland. The Northern Ireland Education Authority Intercultural Education Service and Kitabna - Our Book CIC have been collaborating on multi-lingual children's books welcoming newcomers since 2019, with funding from the UK government's Vulnerable Persons Resettlement Scheme.

Newcomer families in Northern Ireland were asked to share some of their experiences of resettlement to help us identify which themes to address in our stories. Those themes, amongst others, were grief, separation, and trying new things. Our special thanks go to those families for reading our stories ahead of publication, and MaxImpact and the Derry Women's Centre.

About therapeutic stories...

This story is part of a series of three stories created for newcomer communities who may be experiencing grief, seperation and difficulties when trying new things. A therapeutic story uses metaphor to create a safe space in which distressing emotions can be explored and shared. The other stories in this series are:

Where do you come from?
A first new friend

You can find these stories, all additional language versions, and accompanying parent/carer/teacher guides here: www.kitabna.org/therapeutic-stories.html

Once upon a time, in a small cove around the coast from a small fishing village, a furry seal called Soo stared at a small fossil he had carried from home.

It was not just a fossil anyone could find on a beach. This fossil came from the mountains above the beach his family had lived on, before they were all swept away in a storm.

Soo's father told him it was good to hold onto his memories.

"I loved the fish back home," said Soo's father, catching a slippery, silver mackerel between his teeth. "But I can catch fish anywhere. This is our home now, Soo. So I shall catch fish here."

But Soo missed the mountains where the fossil had been found. He could not move those mountains, and like so many seals he knew, they were far, far away from him. Instead he looked at the green hills of his new home, small mountains which became greener and greener with every drop of rain that fell in Northern Ireland. The rain fell almost every day.

Looking at the small mountains made him feel happy sometimes, but sometimes it made him feel all alone, because he felt far from the mountains back home.

But Soo was not alone. One of the small mountains he was watching was watching him too. She had the same sadness in her heart, and one night she decided to tell Soo. Soo heard a whisper in the night, calling him to come to the green hills and climb to the highest point.

6

And so, even though he was a seal, Soo left the next morning, following a muddy path up past the beach and through the fields. He did not tell his mother where he was going. Splish, splash, flap, flop went his flippers! Up he climbed, up, up, up, until he reached the peak and felt the mountain speak softly to him.

"Soo," she said. "I want to show you something. Look out over the sea, to those islands far away."

Soo looked out over the sea and saw the mountains in the distance. They were so far away, the big mountains looked tiny.

"Those mountains were once my friends," the voice said softly. "We lived together and laughed together. And slowly, over time, the land broke and we grew further and further apart. One day we had different lives. The distance grew and grew between us. We stayed in touch but the wind began to carry our voices away. Time made things hard. Now, we can not speak at all."

"I'm sorry," said Soo. "Can you call to them?"

"I don't know how," said the mountain. "I see those wires everywhere, and I hear how humans talk to each other, on telephones. I wish I had a telephone. I have lost my voice. I don't know how you could hear me."

"I also feel very alone sometimes, and far from people I love," said Soo. "Maybe that is why."

Soo left the mountain and went back to his family in the sea, who were very worried about him. The rain had been falling all day, and his fur was covered in sticky, brown mud.

"Soo!" his mother cried as he splashed into their cave. "Where have you been? You should have told the starfish on the door where you were going!"

"I'm sorry, mum," said Soo.

"We missed you," his mum said, hugging him close. "Where were you?"

Soo told his family about the sad mountain who lived above their beach, and asked for their advice.

"I didn't know you were missing home so much," his mother said. "I miss home too. This beach is not the same."

"It's not so bad," said Soo's father, coming in with a big fish between his teeth. "I can catch fish here!"

Suddenly, Soo's sister, Boo, had an idea!

"Now that the mountain has lost her old friends, and we cannot bring them to her, maybe we can just try really hard to be her new friends?" said Boo.

"But how?" said Soo. "How do we be friends with a mountain?"

"Maybe we just have to visit her and spend time together," said Soo. "Remember what Grandmother Seal used to say: sometimes you cannot fix a problem for someone, sometimes you can just be with them, and that can help too."

"Yes, we're new here too!" said their mother. "We could take fish picnics and go up to visit her every weekend."

"And splash at her from the sea!" cried Boo.

"It's a wonderful idea," said Soo's father. "I can collect fish for our picnics!"

"We know you can, dad!" Boo and Soo said together.

And so the family began to visit their new friend, and as time went by, the seagulls, the shells, the crabs and the starfish saw their wonderful adventures going up to the small mountain. Slowly, they started to visit the small mountain too.

The mountain could not replace her friends, but she found in Soo's family a new community, and all of their hearts were happier than they had been in a long time. She would never know this, but over in those distant lands her old mountain friends were missing her too. She hoped the seals helped to take care of them there, and hoped that they also had happiness in their hearts.

More Kitabna stories...

البَطِّيخَةُ العِمْلاقَةُ
The Giant Watermelon

قِصَصُ إِسْرَاء
Esraa's Stories
Written & illustrated by Helen Patuck

عَائِلَةُ القِطِّ
The Cat's Family
Written & illustrated by Helen Patuck

دەریاچەی بۆقەکان
البُحَيرَةُ التي عَاشَتْ فِيها الضَّفادِعُ
The Lake Where Frogs Lived
Written & illustrated by Helen Patuck

سەردانی ڕیشۆڵەکە
زِرْزُورٌ في المُخَيمِ
The Starling's Visit
Written & illustrated by Helen Patuck

كَلِماتُ العَصافِيرِ
The Bird Words
Written and illustrated by Helen Patuck

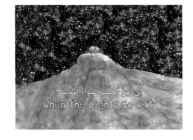

إني أَرى وَجَلتْ أَصْواتُ المُدينةِ
When the Lights Go Out

You can read our stories online for free, and also purchase paperback copies, via our website:

www.kitabna.org

Kitabna – Our Book CIC is a publishing initiative which builds on local storytelling practices and creative peacebuilding to develop safe spaces with communities affected by war. This has manifested in several ways: as multilingual illustrated children's books, story-writing workshops, co-created stories and the development of psychosocial educational tools with INGOs, schools and civil society actors.

Based in London, Kitabna's legal form is a community interest company (CIC), which means we work as a non-profit with communities displaced by conflict in Syria, Lebanon, Israel-Palestine, Turkey, Iraqi Kurdistan, Jordan and across Europe. We have no political or religious affiliation and are self-funded through book sales and consultancies.